P9-BZD-173

WITHDRAWN

THIS IS A GOOD STORY

Story by Adam Lehrhaupt
Pictures by Magali Le Huche

A PAULA WISEMAN BOOK
Simon & Schuster Books for Young Readers
New York London Toronto Sydney New Delhi

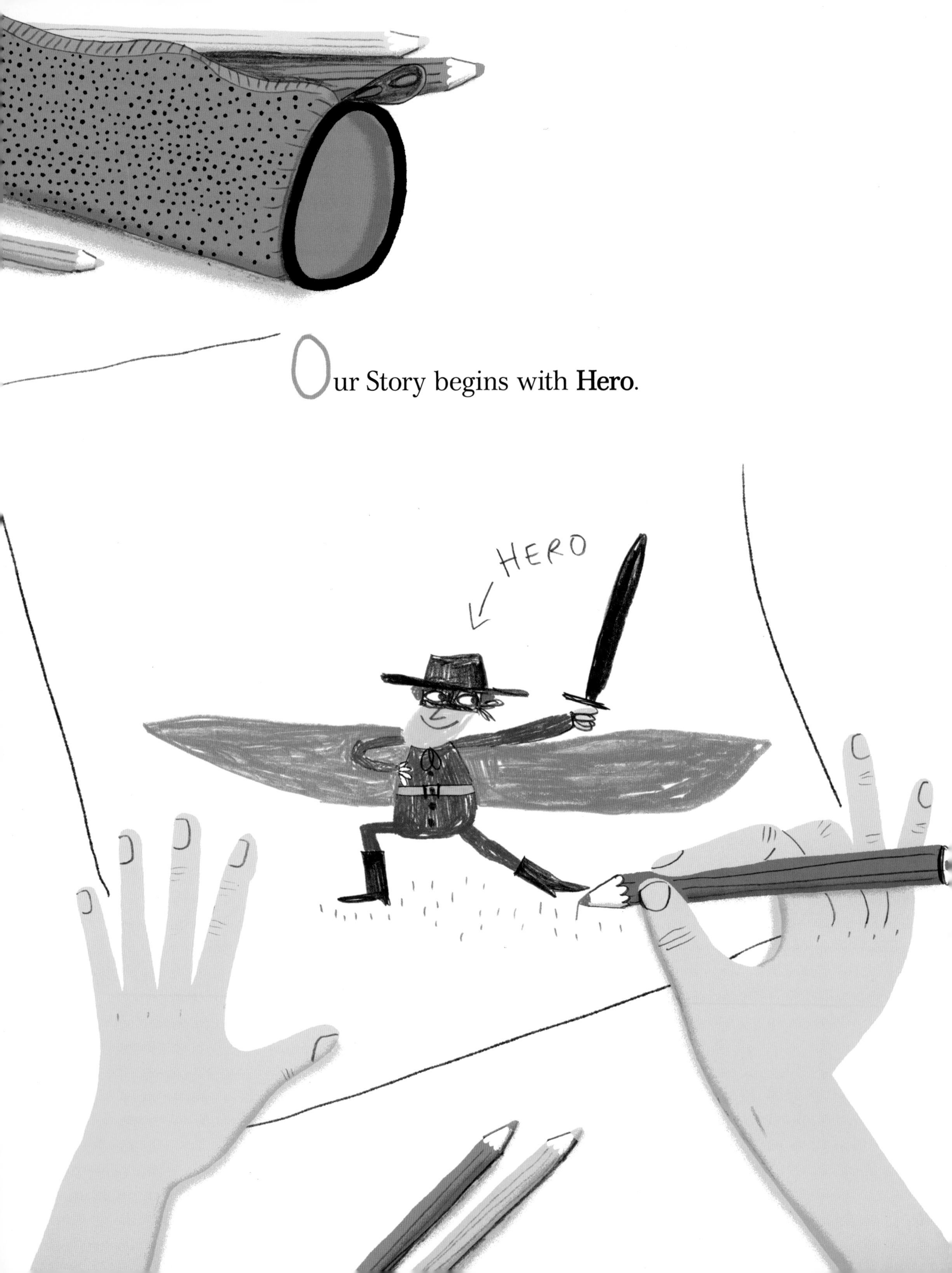

Our Story begins with **Hero**.

Or is it **Heroine**?

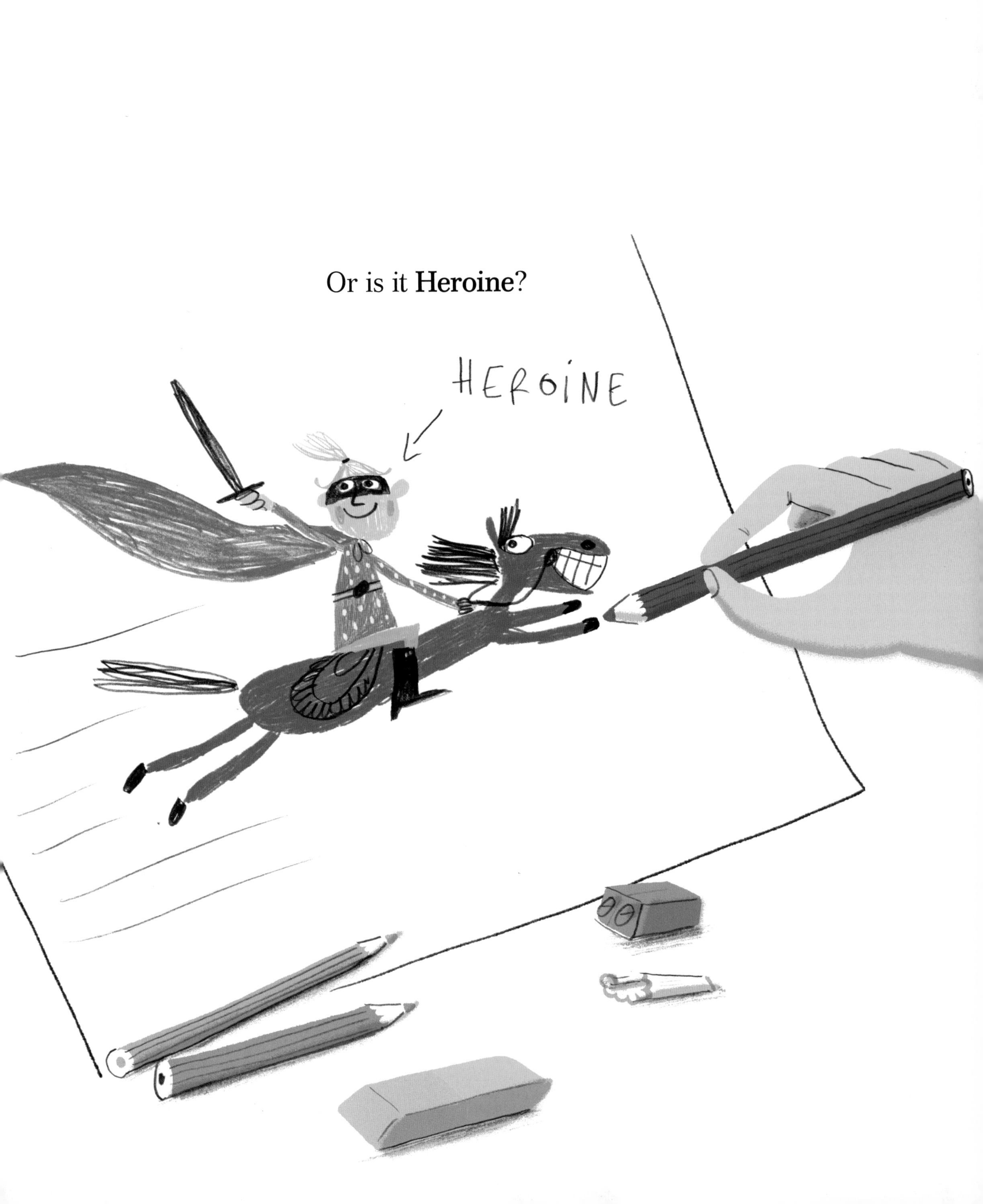

Both?

Yes, that works! Both.

Let's try that again.

Our Story begins with **Hero** *and* **Heroine**.

They live in a good town, filled with good people, called our Setting.

As with any Good Story, ours has a **Conflict**, a problem that needs fixing. And it's a good thing, too, because without a Conflict there would be no **Plot**.

Our Story would go nowhere.

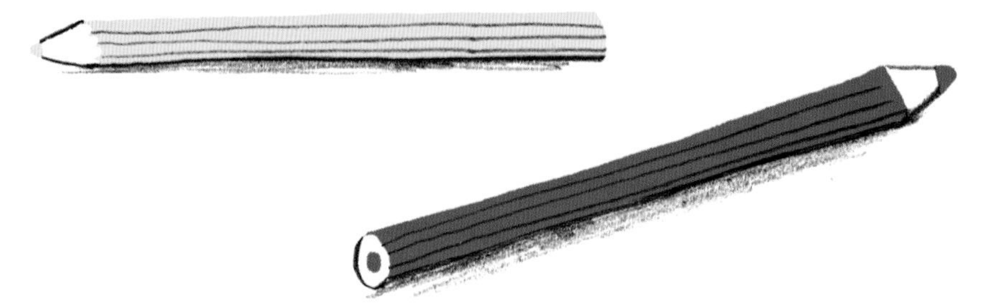

Like it is right now. So . . .

What is the **Conflict** you ask?

Our Setting is under attack!

By a really Bad Guy. And not just any really Bad Guy—

an **Evil Overlord**.

That's not an Evil Overlord!
Come on. That's barely a **Creepy Sidekick**.

Ah, *that's* an Evil Overlord.
Much better. Thank you.

Now, where was I? Right. Under attack.
The people of our Setting fight valiantly, but
Evil Overlord's armies are too numerous.

All the townsfolk are captured . . .

except Hero and Heroine, who just
happen to be rescuing lost ducks
in the town of Very Convenient.

They return to find our Setting empty.
The library is dark.
The candy store is closed!

It is devastating.

closed

Luckily for the captured townsfolk,
Hero and Heroine are people of action.

Seriously? What kind of action is *that*?
This is a dramatic point in the Plot.
Our Conflict is building. The action here will determine the course of the rest of the story.

Try again.

Hero and Heroine dash off to
Evil Lair to rescue the townsfolk.

Unfortunately, Evil Lair is not close.
It's a long, dangerous climb up a dark and
stormy mountain. Up. And up. And . . .

Oh, no! The gate is heavily guarded.
Thinking quickly, Hero distracts the Guard
who turns, trips and . . .

THUNK!

Hero and Heroine
race through Evil Lair.

At last they reach a gate
labeled DUNGEON.

No, no, NO!

Labeled, as in, clearly marked.

With a sign.

This is the most exciting part of the story!

IT'S THE CLIMAX!

Just turn the page.

Hero and Heroine burst into the Dungeon.
The townsfolk cheer.

Hero and Heroine have saved the day!

But not for long.

Uh-oh!

Evil Overlord has returned.

“Head to The End!”

Heroine shouts.

The Final Battle is epic.

They fight to the right. They fight to the left.

Soon, Evil Overlord is surrounded.

There is No Escape.

NO
ESCAPE

THE END
THE END

Victorious, Hero and Heroine join the townsfolk at The End. There is much rejoicing.

Wow! This *is* a Good Story.

Or is it?

* A FRIENDLY LIST OF WORDS USED IN THIS BOOK *

HERO - THE MAIN MALE CHARACTER IN A STORY OR PLAY. THE PROTAGONIST.

HEROINE - THE MAIN FEMALE CHARACTER IN A STORY OR PLAY. THE PROTAGONIST.

PROTAGONIST—(HERO AND HEROINE) THE MAIN CHARACTER, HERO, OR HEROINE IN A STORY OR PLAY.

ANTAGONIST—(EVIL OVERLORD) THE ADVERSARY OF THE PROTAGONIST, HERO, OR HEROINE OF A STORY OR PLAY.

SETTING - THE LOCATION OR TIME IN WHICH THE ACTION OF A STORY OR SCENE TAKES PLACE.

CONFLICT - A CONTROVERSY OR STRUGGLE BETWEEN DIFFERING PRINCIPLES OR INTERESTS.

PLOT - THE MAIN EVENTS IN A STORY OR PLAY.

CLIMAX - A DECISIVE OR INTENSE MOMENT THAT PROVIDES A TURNING POINT FOR THE PLOT.

This heroine is for Alex. Thanks for all you do.
–A. L.

For Clara and Fanette
–M. L. H.

SIMON & SCHUSTER BOOKS FOR YOUNG READERS
An imprint of Simon & Schuster Children's Publishing Division
1230 Avenue of the Americas, New York, New York 10020
Text copyright © 2017 by Adam Lehrhaupt
Illustrations copyright © 2017 by Magali Le Huche
All rights reserved, including the right of reproduction in whole or in part in any form.
SIMON & SCHUSTER BOOKS FOR YOUNG READERS is a trademark of Simon & Schuster, Inc.
For information about special discounts for bulk purchases, please contact Simon & Schuster Special Sales at 1-866-506-1949 or business@simonandschuster.com.
The Simon & Schuster Speakers Bureau can bring authors to your live event. For more information or to book an event, contact the Simon & Schuster Speakers Bureau at 1-866-248-3049 or visit our website at www.simonspeakers.com.
Book design by Krista Vossen
The text for this book was set in Cremona.
The illustrations for this book were rendered in pencil and colored digitally.
Manufactured in China
0617 SCP
First Edition
2 4 6 8 10 9 7 5 3 1
Cataloging-in-Publication Data for this book is available from the Library of Congress.
ISBN 978-1-4814-2935-1
ISBN 978-1-4814-2936-8 (eBook)